J
BROWN
J

# FLAT STANLEY

## The Big Mountain Adventure

DO NOT BEND

## Read all of Flat Stanley's adventures

# FLAT STANLEY

## The Big Mountain Adventure

Created by Jeff Brown

Written by Sara Pennypacker

Illustrated by Jon Mitchell

EGMONT

# EGMONT

*We bring stories to life*

*The Big Mountain Adventure*
First published in Great Britain 2011
by Egmont UK Limited
239 Kensington High Street
London W8 6SA
Text copyright 2011 by the Trust u/w/o Richard C. Brown
a/k/a Jeff Brown f/b/o Duncan Brown
Illustrations copyright 2011 by the Trust u/w/o Richard C. Brown
a/k/a Jeff Brown f/b/o Duncan Brown

ISBN 978 1 4052 5208 9

1 3 5 7 9 10 8 6 4 2

A CIP catalogue record for this title is available from the British Library

Printed and bound in Great Britain by the CPI Group

# CONTENTS

# Chapter One

# Ready, Set . . .

'Sleeping bags?' George Lambchop called out to his wife, Harriet.

'Check!' answered Mrs Lambchop. 'Wholesome snacks for the boys?'

'Check!' replied Mr Lambchop.

The Lambchop family was preparing for their vacation to Mount Rushmore in the Black Hills of South Dakota. They were all very excited about the adventure.

Mr Lambchop was excited because he was going to collect another state park sticker for the rear window of the car.

Mrs Lambchop was excited because she was going to learn more about the history of South Dakota.

Their younger son, Arthur, was excited because he was hoping to meet some real, live cowboys.

And Stanley, the Lambchops' older son, was excited because he was going somewhere nobody would recognise him.

Not long ago, Stanley had awakened to find that his enormous bulletin board had fallen upon him during the night. Since then, the family had got used to having a flattened boy in the house. But when he ventured outside, he often caused a commotion: 'Look, Marge! There he is ... the famous flattened kid! Wonder what new adventure he's up to now?' Or, 'Say there, Flatty, mind if we take a picture?'

The truth is, both Lambchop brothers were a bit tired of all the attention Stanley was getting. It would be nice, they agreed, to go away some place where people didn't make such a fuss.

'Well, I think we're ready,' said Mr Lambchop, surveying the mountain of suitcases and camping equipment in the hall.

'Not quite, dear,' replied Mrs Lambchop. 'Remember, we still have to consult

Doctor Dan about Stanley's travel needs. Better safe than sorry.'

'Well, the boy is still flat,' Doctor Dan pronounced, when he had finished his examination.

'Yes, we know that,' said Stanley's father. 'We were wondering whether such a trip would be suitable for Stanley in his present condition. Mount Rushmore's elevation is 5,725 feet, for one thing. And we'll be travelling by automobile along the scenic highways at a fairly high velocity.'

Here Mrs Lambchop interrupted her husband with a chuckle. 'Not too high a velocity, of course,' she said.

Mr Lambchop smiled at his wife's joke. Both she and Mr Lambchop were always careful to obey local speed limits. 'Still,' he said, 'we did feel it would be wise to check with you.'

'It's a good thing you did. More people should be concerned about the effects of travel on the body. The human being is a very complex organism. Even we doctors, with our extensive knowledge, don't completely understand it.'

'Oh, dear,' Mrs Lambchop said anxiously. 'Will it be all right for Stanley to come with us?'

'Of course!' said Doctor Dan. 'I can't think of any reason why not!'

# Chapter Two

# GO!

The next day, after a hearty breakfast, the Lambchop family began to pack the car for their big trip. In went the tent, four sleeping bags, and the rest of the camping gear. In went the suitcases, the cameras and coolers. Arthur came out with his arms full – his authentic cowboy saddle, his authentic cowboy harmonica and his

authentic cowboy lasso.

'Oh, dear,' Mrs Lambchop murmured, eyeing the overstuffed car. 'There doesn't seem to be much room for the boys!'

'Playing cowboys is for little kids,' Stanley said. 'Now that I've been in the newspaper, I'm too grown-up for that sort of thing. I think Arthur should leave all that stuff behind.'

Arthur glared at his brother. 'Stanley can ride on the roof,' he suggested.

Mr Lambchop considered this. 'Well, if we lash him down securely . . .'

'I think not,' decided Mrs Lambchop. 'We will be pointing out many sights along the way. I don't want Stanley to miss any of them.'

And so both boys squeezed into the backseat with much grumbling, and the family set out.

Along the way, the Lambchops did indeed come upon many wondrous sights: inspiring views, fields with lots of crops, and many other glories of nature.

'We should all be grateful to have good eyesight as we travel through this great land of ours,' Mr Lambchop noted. The rest of the Lambchops agreed they were very fortunate indeed.

Every time they crossed into a new state, the family recited its motto and sang its song. They played Licence Plate Bingo and I Spy, and the hours passed fairly quickly. Nonetheless, everyone was delighted to arrive at the gates of Mount Rushmore State Park. The boys craned their heads out of the windows to gaze up at the sixty-foot-tall faces carved in the mountain, while Mr Lambchop paid the admission fees. And as soon as the car was parked, they sprang out.

'I'm all crumpled!' Stanley complained, trying to smooth himself out.

'Well, I'm practically flattened!' grumbled Arthur.

'Boys, hurry along,' said Mrs Lambchop. 'We're just in time to catch the last tour group.'

The Lambchops fell in with a group

of cheerful-looking tourists. 'In nineteen thirty-seven,' the tour guide was telling them, 'a bill was introduced to add

Susan B. Anthony as a fifth face. This bill failed, so today we still have the original four presidents: Washington,

Jefferson, Roosevelt and Lincoln, who is directly below us now.'

Mr and Mrs Lambchop were fascinated by the interesting facts the tour guide related. But the boys wandered away from the group – they were still feeling a little rambunctious after spending so many hours cramped in the car.

They were also still feeling, it must be said, a little irritable with each other.

'Ha, ha!' Arthur taunted his brother from the edge of the mountain. 'I can stand right out here, but you can't! You'd blow away now that you're flat!'

Suddenly, the ground shook.

'Arthur!' Stanley cried. 'You'd better come ba–'

With a terrible sound, a large crack split open along Abraham Lincoln's hairline. The great carved face began to slide away down the mountainside . . . with Arthur on it!

Without thinking of his own safety, Stanley lunged out and grabbed hold of the retreating rock face. He held on tightly. 'Climb over me!' he called to his brother. 'Use me as a bridge!'

Arthur did. In a moment he was back on firm ground, where Mr and Mrs Lambchop ran to embrace him.

Just then, a park ranger appeared.

'You! Flat Boy! Can you hold on a little longer?' he called out to Stanley. 'The repair crew is on the way.'

Mr and Mrs Lambchop were indignant. 'My son has a name,' Mrs Lambchop said. 'He is called Stanley!'

'Sorry, ma'am,' the ranger said. 'I should have known better, because the same thing happens to me, too. My name is Bob, as it says right here on my name badge. But to park visitors I'm always just "Hey, ranger!" It makes me feel very bad, indeed, as you can imagine.'

Mrs Lambchop forgave Bob, but Mr Lambchop was still indignant. 'Stanley is one of those park visitors. He paid an entrance fee, just like everyone else here.

I really don't think you should ask anything from him.'

'I'm afraid we don't have any choice, Sir,' Ranger Bob replied. 'The stakes are simply too high.'

So Stanley held on until the emergency crew arrived to repair the crack. Only then did he let go. When he righted himself, he was surprised by a sea of flashing lightbulbs.

A reporter thrust a microphone in his face. '"The boy who saved Mount Rushmore!"' one reporter crowed. 'That will be my headline for the evening edition!'

'"Brave Boy Becomes Big Band-Aid!"' cried another.

Off to the side, Arthur crossed his arms over his cowboy vest and frowned. 'Famous again,' he grumbled. 'And nobody knows who I am!'

As soon as the reporters left, Stanley rejoined his brother in the large group that had gathered. Everyone was talking about the strange earthquake that had just happened.

'That warn't no earthquake,' muttered a voice behind the boys. 'That was a gold mine!'

Stanley and Arthur turned to see a girl about Stanley's age, scowling.

She was wearing a worn leather vest and chaps, and dusty boots with big silver spurs.

The boys introduced themselves.

'Good to meet you, pardner,' the girl answered. 'I'm the tour guide's daughter. The name's Calamity Jasper.'

# Chapter Three

# Calamity Jasper

The tourists dispersed, but Stanley and Arthur hung back with the cowgirl.

'What did you mean just then – about it not being an earthquake?' asked Stanley.

Calamity spread her arms out to the mountain range around them. 'Thar's gold in them thar hills,' she said. 'Everyone knows about the gold rush of the eighteen seventies. Rumour is there's still more in those abandoned mines. I reckon someone's dynamiting to get to it.'

'Gold?' Arthur repeated. 'Real gold in a real gold mine?'

'Yep,' Calamity answered. 'I'm about to get me some myself. I found a map.'

Stanley and Arthur looked at each other. 'Can we come, too?' they blurted out at the same time.

Calamity Jasper yanked her hat down and squinted up at the boys. 'Okeydoke,' she decided at last. 'I reckon you fellas could tag along. Might be needing some extra hands if I find a really big vein.'

The next morning, the Lambchop family

awakened in their tent to the sound of birdsong and the scent of piney woods. Everyone was eager to begin the day, but Mrs Lambchop insisted they wait for a good breakfast.

'It's the most important meal of the day,' she said to her family. She was such a skilful cook that she made an excellent breakfast over the little campfire using only the tinned and dried provisions they had packed. The Lambchops ate with the hearty appetites brought on by outdoor living, and then they tidied the campsite. Just as the sleeping bags were being rolled up, a rustling at the tent flap caught their attention.

Calamity Jasper strode inside. 'Time for

all the young'uns to report to powwow!' she announced to Mr and Mrs Lambchop. She winked to Stanley and Arthur.

'Did you hear that, George?' exclaimed Mrs Lambchop. 'What a wonderful tour . . . so much for the boys to do!'

'Can we go?' asked Arthur and Stanley, excited.

'It's "may we go", dears,' Mrs Lambchop corrected her sons. 'We are not on a vacation from proper speech.' Then she sent a questioning look to her husband.

'Sounds like a fine plan to me!' Mr Lambchop said.

So the boys eagerly followed Calamity Jasper to her horse.

'This here's Gold Rush, my trusty steed,'

she said, patting a beautiful palomino.
'Arthur, you can ride up on the saddle
behind me. And you, hmm . . .' She eyed
Stanley thoughtfully.

'I'll roll you like a blanket and tie you on behind, right here under the cantle. That all right with you, buckaroo?'

'Oh, sure,' Stanley said. 'I am very limber.' He showed her how he could bend and fold himself about, although normally he was much more modest about his abilities.

'Me, too,' Arthur chimed in. 'I am very limber, too.' And he did a couple of somersaults in front of the cowgirl.

'Also, I am very good at holding on,' Stanley said. 'Remember yesterday? How I held on to Lincoln's face?'

Arthur stepped in front of his brother, holding out his lasso and his harmonica. 'Well,' he said, 'I have a lot of authentic cowboy gear.'

'Time's a-wastin',' Calamity said, shaking her head at the boys. She rolled Stanley up, being careful to leave his head sticking out, and lashed him to the saddle. Then she stuck one boot into a stirrup and swung herself on to her horse. Last, she pulled Arthur up behind her. 'Giddyap!' she called to Gold Rush, and they were off.

Trotting along the trail was very pleasant. The Lambchop boys, being from a big city, were delighted to be out in so much nature. To pass the time, Calamity taught them cowboy songs, about painful longings for home, faithful horses and wide-open spaces. Things like that.

The children were surprised to find that their voices were in perfect harmony, soaring and twining in the clear mountain air with astonishing beauty. Probably, in fact, three people had never sung cowboy songs that beautifully before. If a talent scout had happened to hear them that day, he would have signed them up to a record contract on the spot. But that's not what happened. What happened was they ran out of songs.

After that, Calamity pointed out the plants and animals along the trail. They saw pine and spruce trees and many wildflowers. They saw prairie dogs, red squirrels, deer and even a herd of bison in the distance.

'Mountain lions are native here, too,' Calamity said.

'And look,' said Stanley. 'Mountain goats!'

'They're not native, though,' Calamity Jasper told the boys. 'In nineteen twenty-four, Canada gave Custer State Park six goats. They escaped their pen and began to live in the wild. There are about two hundred of them now.'

Calamity was an excellent guide, and the boys were interested in all the things she told them as they rode along. But after a while, what they were really interested in was getting to the gold mine.

At last they did.

# Into the Mine!

Stanley and Arthur waited impatiently while Calamity Jasper led Gold Rush to a shady spot by a stream, so he could drink and munch grass. Then they followed her to the mine entrance.

Calamity handed each boy a flashlight. Then she switched on her headlamp and led them in. The mine was dark and dank.

When their eyes adjusted, the boys could make out several men, blackened with dirt, chipping away at the walls and whispering to one another.

'Don't pay them any mind,' Calamity whispered. 'Them prospectors are a jealous bunch. Every man to himself, that kind of thing. They'll hog-tie you and throw you off the mountain if they think you're trespassing on to their claims.' She nodded into the darkness. 'Reckon we better mosey on a little further.'

The boys followed Calamity deeper and deeper into the dark mine shaft. The tink-tink-tink of the hammers grew fainter and fainter, and the light grew dimmer and dimmer.

'I don't see any gold yet!' Arthur called out to Calamity Jasper, who was far ahead now.

'Right! Where's the gold?' Stanley called out even louder.

The boys were comforted by their voices in the dark, dank mine. 'Where's the gold?' they cried together.

'Don't yell,' came Calamity's voice. 'You'll cause a —'

Suddenly, there was a tremendous rumbling roar! Rocks and rubble came crashing down in front of Stanley and Arthur . . . a cave-in! So that was why everyone was whispering!

At the mine's entrance, the prospectors dropped their hammers and ran out.

'Every man for himself!' they cried. 'Head for the hills!'

Stanley was tempted to call after them that they were already in the hills. But he was much too worried to be bothered.

'Where's Calamity Jasper?' he asked Arthur.

The boys played their flashlights over the wall of rocks and dirt in front of them. 'Do you think –' Arthur whispered.

'Shhh,' Stanley whispered back.

In the quiet, the boys could make out a muffled voice: 'Gol-durned . . . gol-durned . . . gol-durned fools!'

'Don't worry, Calamity,' Stanley called – quietly – to the trapped cowgirl.

'We'll get you out of there.'

'Step aside,' Arthur told his brother. 'It's your fault she's in there.' Then he called to Calamity — quietly also, 'I'll get you out. I'm very strong for my age.'

Arthur was strong, that was true. But it was also true that he felt a lot stronger when he was wearing his Mighty Man T-shirt. And today he was wearing his authentic cowboy clothes instead.

He pushed against a big rock. He pushed and he pushed. The rock didn't budge.

'Step aside,' Stanley said. 'It's your fault she's in there. I'll get her out with my flatness.'

Stanley surveyed the rubble in front of him. There was a gap between two big

rocks about an inch wide.
It might work!

He squeezed and folded
himself until . . . yes! Stanley
Lambchop worked himself
through until he came out
into a small clear space . . .
and there was Calamity,
sitting on a rock.

'I'm here!' he said proudly. 'You can stop worrying now!'

Calamity looked up at him. 'And why's that?'

'Because I'm used to being a hero. It's what I do, now that I am flat. I rescued my mother's favourite ring, and I helped capture sneak thieves at the Famous Museum. So I'll get you out,' he assured her.

Calamity Jasper stood up and turned her head so her headlamp lit up the small space. 'Really?' she asked. 'How?'

Stanley looked around. He saw the problem: he could get through the gap in the rocks, but she couldn't. 'I'm sorry,' he said, embarrassed. 'I'll come up with something.'

'Just go get help,' Calamity muttered. Then she sat down on the rock and turned her back to him.

Stanley worked himself through to the other side again.

'My flatness didn't help,' he admitted to Arthur.

'Well, my strength didn't help either,' Arthur said. 'Too bad we couldn't combine the two – hey!' He jumped up. 'We've been studying machines at school! Do you know how a lever works?'

Stanley understood Arthur's clever idea at once. The boys rolled a small rock beside the larger one, and Stanley lay himself over it. He worked his feet under the large rock and made himself stiff as a board. 'Use your strength to press down on my shoulders,' he directed his brother.

Arthur did. With a deep creak, the boulder rolled aside!

Calamity Jasper crawled through the gap. She narrowed her eyes and scowled at the two boys as she stormed past them to the mine entrance.

The boys followed, and after the three children rubbed their eyes in the bright afternoon sunshine, they stared in disbelief: Gold Rush was gone!

# On the Trail

'Must-a been spooked by the cave-in,' Calamity moaned. 'I'll have to track him before he gets too far!'

The boys kept a safe distance behind – Calamity didn't seem in any mood for their company. Now and then they heard her muttering, 'Gol-durned show-offs!' and they dropped back even further.

Stanley and Arthur felt miserable. They had been show-offs, and they knew it now.

After a while, Calamity gave a little whoop and ran into a clearing. There stood Gold Rush, snorting and lathered with sweat. The cowgirl threw her arms around her horse. 'Let's get you some water, fella,' she said.

Calamity looked around. 'We're a ways off from the stream,' she said out loud. 'And I don't see any signs of a spring . . .'

'I can help! I have an idea!' Stanley cried.

Calamity shot him a look that said she'd heard just about enough from him. But Stanley did indeed have an idea.

He lay down in the grass in front of Gold Rush and curved himself into the shape of a trough. 'Pour in some water from the canteens,' he directed Calamity.

Calamity did, and then Stanley held very still as the horse's big lips came right down and slurped from his belly. It tickled, but Stanley Lambchop did not move. And he did not spill one drop.

When Gold Rush had finished drinking, Calamity helped Stanley to his feet. She wore a big grin as she shook his hand. 'Maybe I was wrong about you, pardner,' she said. 'Any friend of my horse is a friend of mine.'

'So you're not angry with us any more?' asked Arthur.

'Shucks, no. I reckon you two aren't half bad for a couple of greenhorns. Now I better fix us some grub. We are lost, pardners. We're gonna have to figure out how we get home from here. A cowboy can't think on an empty stomach.'

Calamity Jasper pulled a can of beans and a pot from her saddlebags. She built a fire, and soon the beans were bubbling cheerfully in the pot. 'Cowboys always carry beans for emergencies,' she confided.

Arthur made a mental note to carry beans with him from now on. 'How did you learn to be a cowboy?' he asked Calamity. 'How did you learn to follow tracks like that? We didn't see anything, but you followed them right to Gold Rush.'

'Following tracks isn't a cowboy skill. I'm part Lakota Sioux,' Calamity said proudly. 'We Native Americans know lots of useful things, like which plants make medicine and how to hunt and fish and how to use – Whoa, doggie! Smoke signals!'

Calamity jumped to her feet. She ordered Arthur to gather a load of tumbleweeds. When he returned, she piled the tumbleweeds on to the campfire. Immediately, a dark thick smoke streamed upward.

'What about a blanket?' Stanley asked. 'Don't you need a blanket for smoke signals?'

Calamity grinned. 'That's where you come in, pardner!'

Both boys understood at once.

Arthur picked up Stanley's foot, and Calamity took hold of his arm. Together, they flapped Stanley over the fire, sending puffs of thick smoke into the clear air. Stanley very bravely held his breath and didn't cough once.

Before too long, they heard a rustling in the bushes at the edge of the clearing. The tour group!

'We saw the signals,' Calamity's father said. 'Came to see what you youngsters were up to.'

'Looks like they're up to a real Wild West time!' said George Lambchop. 'What a trip, eh, boys?'

Chapter Six

# Around the Campfire

The children were grateful to follow the tour group back along the trail. As they crested Mount Rushmore over Lincoln's face, the boys walked to the edge to take a look. The repair crew had done an excellent job. The crack was barely visible.

Stanley stepped out even further. 'See, Arthur,' he boasted. 'See, I can stand out here too! It's easy!'

But just then a sudden gust of wind caught Stanley by surprise. It swept him off his feet, and he went skittering down Lincoln's steep forehead, coming to rest on the bridge of Lincoln's long nose!

Stanley held on for dear life. He looked around . . . far, far above him he saw Arthur, looking terribly worried. And suddenly he was very glad his brother had brought his authentic cowboy gear with him . . .

'Arthur!' he cried. 'Throw down your lasso!'

Arthur uncoiled his lasso and swung it around and around, aiming. Then he let go, and the rope went sailing out

into the South Dakota sky . . . and landed right in front of Stanley's outstretched hand!

Calamity Jasper gave Arthur an admiring nod. 'Mighty fine twirling, buckaroo!' she applauded. 'Mighty fine.'

Stanley grabbed hold of the rope and tied it around his waist. 'Bring me up, Arthur!' he called.

Just then, another gust of wind blew across the mountain. It lifted Stanley Lambchop up like a kite, up and up until the lasso was stretched taut. Stanley flew high above the tour group!

'Boys!' Mrs Lambchop called, when she saw what was going on. 'Quit all that horsing around right now!'

'Now dear, the boys are just having a bit of fun,' Mr Lambchop said. 'It's their vacation, after all. I don't see the harm.'

'I suppose you're right, George,' Mrs Lambchop said.

'Still, I noticed Stanley smelled strongly of smoke, and that is not good for a growing boy. I'd like him to come back to camp and change his clothes. Arthur, reel your brother in now, please.'

When Stanley was back on earth, Mr Lambchop invited Calamity to join them for a cookout. After a delicious meal of hot dogs and hamburgers, Mrs Lambchop said, 'I believe this celebration calls for marshmallow s'mores!' to cheers all around.

While they were busy toasting the marshmallows, Stanley and Arthur apologised for causing so much trouble in the mine earlier. 'Also, we're sorry you didn't find any gold,' Arthur said. 'You have nothing to show for all that time in the mine.'

'Well, that ain't exactly so, pardner,' Calamity said with a grin. She dug into her pocket and produced a large gleaming gold nugget. 'I found it in my boot. Reckon it fell there during the cave-in.'

'Real gold!' breathed Arthur. 'Can I hold it?'

'You can do more than hold it, pardner,' Calamity said with a mysterious smile. 'You got a hammer?'

Arthur fetched the hammer they had packed to pound in the tent stakes.

Calamity placed the nugget on a flat rock and brought the hammer down hard, cracking it into three chunks of gold. She gave one to Stanley and one to Arthur.

'They're yours, you earned it,' she said

to the brothers. 'Way I see it, without the cave-in, I wouldn't have had the gold in the first place. And without you, there wouldn't have been no cave-in.'

And with that, Calamity Jasper mounted her trusty steed, waved goodbye, and rode off into the sunset.

# Chapter Seven

# There's No Place Like Home

The next day was the last day of their vacation. Calamity was off at a rodeo, and the Lambchops were enjoying the park as a family. Many interesting activities filled the day, but Mr and Mrs Lambchop noticed the boys seemed subdued.

'It's the lack of fresh vegetables and fruit,

George,' Mrs Lambchop fretted back at the campsite that afternoon.

'I dare say you're right, dear,' Mr Lambchop said. 'You know the boys so well.'

Just as they were packing up, a park ranger strode into their camp.

'Why, hello there, Bob,' Mrs Lambchop greeted him, remembering how he felt about his name.

'Hello, Lambchops,' Ranger Bob said. 'Sure are sorry to see you folks go.'

'We've had a grand time,' Mr Lambchop told him. 'Worth every penny of our admission fees!'

'That's why I'm here,' said Ranger Bob. 'I've been thinking about what you said,

and you were right. Your brave son Stanley paid his fee like everyone else, and given what a hero he was, something doesn't seem right about that. You've taught me a lesson . . . I'm here to refund that fee, with the park's gratitude!'

'Excuse me,' Stanley interrupted politely, 'but my brother was a hero, too. If it weren't for him being out there, I would never have grabbed on to the face of that rock.'

'I can see how that is,' agreed the ranger. 'Two heroes, two refunds it is!'

Then Ranger Bob personally affixed the Mount Rushmore State Park sticker to the rear window of the Lambchops' car, and bade them a safe trip home.

Mrs Lambchop looked into the car, overstuffed once more. 'I'm sorry, boys, but . . .'

'No,' said Stanley. 'Arthur can have the space. You can mail me home. I don't mind.'

So the Lambchops drove to the nearest post office and slipped their elder son into a large mailing envelope, along with the rest of the graham crackers, a slice of American cheese, and a deck of cards.

'Insurance?' asked the postmaster.

Mr Lambchop chuckled as if the postmaster had made a good joke. 'No need. There's no finer postal system in the world. I say, if you can't trust the United States Postal Service to deliver a package safely, then whom can you trust?'

Mrs Lambchop asked that the envelope be marked Fragile, but Stanley was horrified at that suggestion. He did allow the postmaster to stamp Do Not Bend, however.

And then the four Lambchops made their way home from South Dakota: three of them in a car, and one in postal trucks and planes.

Stanley arrived home first, refreshed by his restful trip, and helped unpack the car when his weary family appeared.

'It's always good to get away,' Mr Lambchop noted with a sigh. 'But . . .'

'But it's always good to get back home,' finished his wife.

Then Stanley and Arthur hurried to their room to unpack, while their parents tended to the stack of mail that had piled up.

Arthur pinned the newspaper article about them up on the bulletin board. 'Brother Heroes!' read the headline above a photo of the boys smiling with their arms around each other. 'You know, Stanley,' he said, 'I don't think I ever thanked you for

what you did – becoming a bridge for me to cross over.'

'Well, I didn't thank you either, for lassoing me when I fell down the mountain,' Stanley replied. He unpacked the two gold nuggets and placed them on the bookcase. 'Brotherhood is more important than gold!'

'Right!' agreed Arthur. 'And it's more important than any girl too! Even a cowgirl!'

'Right,' said Stanley. 'Brothers above all!'

'Boys, there's a postcard here,' Mrs Lambchop's voice interrupted them. 'It's from Calamity Jasper.'

'For me!' Stanley and Arthur each cried at the same time.

'It's addressed to Cowpoke Lambchop,' their mother called out. 'I'll leave it here in the hall.'

In their haste to see it, Stanley and Arthur, the brothers above all, nearly trampled each other running out of their room.

Turn the page to read about
Stanley's Great Egyptian
Adventure . . .

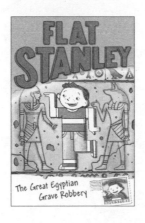

The Great Egyptian
Grave Robbery

Chapter One

# A Letter for Stanley

George Lambchop was sitting at the kitchen table, going through the mail as his wife cooked breakfast. 'Look at these beauties, Harriet!' he called, holding up a letter with many exotic stamps in the corner. 'From Egypt!'

Ever since their eldest son, Stanley, had been flattened by a bulletin board and could now travel by mail, the Lambchop family had become keenly interested in stamps.

'In a minute, dear,' Mrs Lambchop said. 'I'm just at the difficult part of flipping this French toast. A letter from Egypt, you say! Why don't you open it and read it to me.'

Mr Lambchop began to do just that, but he caught himself in time. 'That was a close one!' he cried. 'Do you know it's a federal offence to open mail that's addressed to someone else. This letter is for Stanley!'

Just then, both the Lambchop boys appeared in the kitchen doorway, drawn by the delicious breakfast aroma of

French toast and bacon.

'Stanley, son, letter for you here. Looks important.'

'What about me?' Stanley's younger brother, Arthur, asked. 'Any mail for me today?'

'Not today, sorry,' Mr Lambchop replied. 'But, Stanley, why don't you open yours and read it to us over breakfast?'

'*After* breakfast,' Mrs Lambchop said firmly. '*And* hand washing. You know how maple syrup gets all over everything.'

The boys finished their breakfast and washed up. Then Stanley opened his letter.

'If you are the world-famous flattened boy of America,' he read out loud, 'and if you are less than three inches thick, you must come to Egypt at once. We are beginning an archeological project and are in urgent need of someone of your dimensions.'

'I don't know about *world-famous*,' Arthur grumbled – a bit enviously, it must be said. 'Maybe they've got the wrong person.'

'But I *am* only half an inch thick.' Stanley sighed. 'So that's me, all right.'

'*I*,' Mrs Lambchop corrected her son. 'That is *I*.'

'It's signed Sir Abu Shenti Hawara the Fourth,' Stanley said. 'And look: he's taken care of my travel arrangements.' Stanley held up a very large envelope covered with stamps.

George Lambchop took the letter and read it over. 'No mention of Stanley's *family* going with him,' he said, frowning. 'I don't know . . .'

'Well, an archaeological project . . . it's not as if it's something dangerous.

And travel *is* broadening, George . . .'
Mrs Lambchop mused. 'Oh, Stanley,
darling . . . I didn't mean it that way!
What I meant was, it rounds out one's
education . . . oh my, that didn't come
out quite right either!'

'Well, your mother and I have always
encouraged you boys to lend a helping
hand when needed,' Mr Lambchop said.
'I suppose that goes even if it's needed
halfway around the world.'

'We'd better take you to the post
office at once, Stanley,' Mrs Lambchop
said. 'I will pack the leftover French
toast and bacon for you to eat on the
way. No maple syrup, of course. It
wouldn't do to arrive all sticky!'

'Something to drink?' Stanley asked.

'I think not, dear,' his mother told him. 'Egypt is quite a distance, and I'm afraid you won't be near a bathroom for some time. Which reminds me . . .' And she went off to pack a toothbrush and facecloth for her son's trip.

Stanley noticed that Arthur seemed glum. He knew Arthur sometimes found it difficult being the only round brother in the family. 'Would you like me to bring back something from Egypt for you?' he asked.

'Hmmmph,' Arthur replied. 'If you're going to Egypt, you should bring me back a mummy.'

'I don't believe they offer those as

souvenirs. And besides, it wouldn't fit in the envelope with Stanley!' chuckled the boys' father. Mr Lambchop was known for his sharp sense of humour. 'How about a nice postcard?' Mr Lambchop was known for being a practical thinker, too.

Arthur folded his hands across his chest. 'A mummy or nothing . . .'

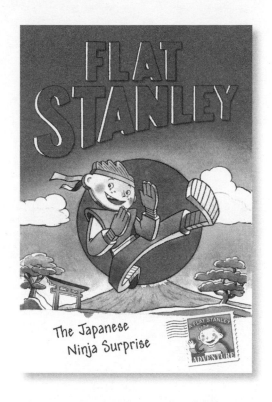

The Japanese
Ninja Surprise

## Whoever heard of a flat ninja?

Stanley is a huge fan of the ninja movie star
Oda Nobu. So he decides to send something
even better than fan mail – himself!

Soon enough, Flat Stanley is in Japan with
Oda Nobu. But trouble is not far behind.
Lucky that they have their ninja moves!

# Read all of Flat Stanley's adventures!

## EGMONT PRESS: ETHICAL PUBLISHING

Egmont Press is about turning writers into successful authors and children into passionate readers – producing books that enrich and entertain. As a responsible children's publisher, we go even further, considering the world in which our consumers are growing up.

### Safety First
Naturally, all of our books meet legal safety requirements. But we go further than this; every book with play value is tested to the highest standards – if it fails, it's back to the drawing-board.

### Made Fairly
We are working to ensure that the workers involved in our supply chain – the people that make our books – are treated with fairness and respect.

### Responsible Forestry
We are committed to ensuring all our papers come from environmentally and socially responsible forest sources.

**For more information, please visit our website at
www.egmont.co.uk/ethical**